# THE DAY OF
# AHMED'S SECRET

## FLORENCE PARRY HEIDE
## & JUDITH HEIDE GILLILAND

ILLUSTRATED BY TED LEWIN

LONDON · VICTOR GOLLANCZ LTD · 1991

Judy girl: See? Anything is possible!

F. P. H.

Mom: You always believed and you were right.

J. H. G.

In memory of John Dickey

T.L.

*Butagaz is a word used to refer to butane gas canisters used
in gas stoves.*

*Rose-water is water in which rose petals have been steeped.*

Text copyright © 1990 by Florence Parry Heide and Judith Heide Gilliland
Illustrations copyright © 1990 by Ted Lewin

The right of Florence Parry Heide, Judith Heide Gilliland and Ted Lewin to be identified as authors of this work
has been asserted by them in accordance with the Copyright, Designs and Patents Act 1988

First published in the USA 1990
by Lothrop, Lee & Shepard Books, a division of William Morrow & Co, Inc.

First published in Great Britain 1991
by Victor Gollancz Ltd,
14 Henrietta Street, London WC2E 8QJ

Printed and bound in Hong Kong by Imago Publishing Ltd

A CIP catalogue record for this book is available from the British Library

ISBN 0-575-05079-9

oday I have a secret, and all day long my secret will be like a friend to me.

Tonight I will tell it to my family, but now I have work to do in my city.

My donkey pulls the cart I ride on. I have many stops to make
today. The streets are crowded. Everyone is going somewhere.
Like me, everyone has something important to do.
And they are making such a noise of it!

All kinds of sounds, maybe every sound in the world, are tangled together: trucks and donkeys, cars and camels, carts and buses, dogs and bells, shouts and calls and whistles and laughter all at once.

I have a sound, too, the sound my cart makes: *Karink rink rink, karink rink rink.* I know my sound helps to make the whole sound of the city, and it would not be the same without me.

Loudest of all to me today is the silent sound of my secret, which I have not yet spoken.

Over all the noise I hear my name, "Ahmed! Ahmed!" And my name becomes part of the city sound too.

It is Hassan calling to me. He leans over the counter of his cart, and the bright colours of the cart mingle with the other colours of the street, the way the noises all go together to make the sound of the city.

My special colours are part of the city, too. Woven into the harness of my donkey are my own good-luck ones, blue, green, and gold.

Hassan hands me a dish of beans and noodles and says, "And how goes the day of my friend the butagaz boy?"

As I eat, Hassan and I laugh together at his jokes and stories. Always when I come home at sundown I tell his stories to my family, but tonight will be different. I will have my secret to tell them. I have been saving it until tonight.

Now someone else comes to Hassan's cart and I wave goodbye. I must hurry now if I am to get all my work finished today.

The first place I go is the home of the old woman. She has been waiting for me.

"Ahmed! Ahmed!" she calls. "Are you bringing me the fuel for my stove?"

The old woman is leaning out of her window. I look up and smile. I am proud that I can carry these big heavy bottles all the way up the steps to the floor where she lives. I am proud that I can do this work to help my family.

I make more stops, and now I am hungry again. I look for the bright red and yellow cart where I can buy my lunch, and I find it in its usual place near the old building.

I buy my beans and rice, and sit in the shade of the old wall.

My father has told me the wall is a thousand years old, and even our great-great-grandfathers were not yet born when it was built. There are many old buildings, many old walls like the one I lean against, in this city.

I close my eyes and have my quiet time, the time my father says I must have each day. "If there are no quiet spaces in your head, it fills with noise," he has told me.

He has shown me how to find my way in the city, and he has taken me to each place where I now have to bring the heavy bottles.

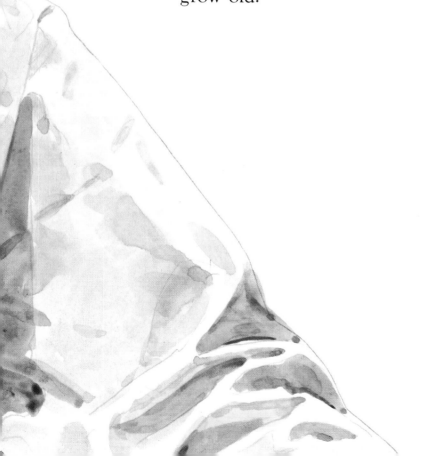

In those days before I was strong enough to do this work alone, I would sit in the cart and watch my father lift and carry the bottles. One day I told him that now I could do it by myself. He watched me try to take a heavy bottle from the cart. I could not do it, and I was ashamed.

"Hurry to grow strong, Ahmed," my father said on that day. For the first time I saw that his face had a tired look, like the faces of the old men in the city.

"Hurry to grow strong," he said again. "But do not hurry to grow old."

Now as I lean against the old building, I think of the sea of sand that lies along our city. I have seen it, stretching as far as the wind.

My father says the wind carries sand all through the city to remind us that the desert is there, is there beside us, and is a part of us.

He tells me that the great desert presses against our city on one side, and the great river pushes against it on the other.

"We live between them," my father has said. "Between our two friends, the river and the desert."

All over the world, people know of our city, he tells me, and they speak its name: Cairo. And they say the name of our great river, the Nile.

"And the desert, what is that called?" I ask.

My father shrugs and smiles. "The hot winds call our desert home."

He himself has never crossed the desert. But in the city are the caravans of camels and their riders who have crossed it many times, the way the boats cross and re-cross the river.

I lean against the wall and I think of these things and of my secret, but I must finish my work before I go home.

First I try to knock the sand from my sandals. The sand is a part of each day, like the noise, like the colours of the city, like the things my father has said.

On the way to my next stop I see the boy who carries bread.

From a window a girl lowers a basket to him on a rope, and he puts some bread in the basket. Like me, he has many stops to make each day, but he is not strong enough to do what I do. No one lowers a rope to me for my heavy loads! No rope could carry what I carry.

I hear the rose-water man before I see him. He clicks two cups together as he walks along the street so people will hear him and come to him for a drink.

I give him my smile. He does not give me his, but our eyes meet and we know we are connected to the same day and to the city.

I do not buy his rose-water, but seeing him has reminded me how hot and thirsty I am. I take a drink from the bottle of water I always carry in my cart.

There are more stops to make, and more times up and up narrow steps with my heavy load, and then I am back in my cart.

*Karink rink rink, karink rink rink.*

It is a long day. I think the moment will never come when I may share my secret, but of course I know that each day ends and that every moment has its time to be.

Finally I am home. It is sundown, it is the time of day when you cannot tell a white thread from a black one. My mother has already lighted the lanterns. Everyone is waiting for me.

Instead of telling them about my day, I say, "Look, I have something to show you."

It is time to tell my secret. I take a deep breath.

"Look," I say. "Look, I can write my name."

I write my name over and over as they watch, and I think of my name now lasting longer than the sound of it, maybe even lasting, like the old buildings in the city, a thousand years.